Disney · PIXAR
ONWARD

Ian & Barley's
Magical Book
of Jokes, Puns, and Gags

Written by Steve Behling
Illustrated by the Disney Storybook Art Team

DISNEP PRESS
Los Angeles · New York

Printed in the United States of America

First Paperback Edition, February 2020

1   3   5   7   9   10   8   6   4   2

Library of Congress Control Number: 2019949152

ISBN 978-1-368-06163-6

FAC-029261-19361

For more Disney Press fun, visit www.disneybooks.com

Barley: BEHOLD!

Ian: You are about to take a bold step into the strange and wondrous world of...

JOKES!

Barley: And riddles!

Ian: Sure, and riddles, too!

Barley: Oh! And puns! Don't forget the puns!

Ian: There are plenty of puns inside.

Barley: Gags about trash unicorns! What about those?

Ian: I think that's covered under "jokes."

Barley: Not specifically, it isn't.

Ian: *Sigh* Anyway, turn the page, and prepare to be amused!

Contents

Magic, Mayhem, and More

What kind of gem can teach you to read?

A *Phonics* Gem!

What's the smelliest kind of candy?

Sparkle Stinks!

What position does Officer Bronco play in basketball?

Centaur!

What do you call a really dull adventure?

A Quest of *Bore*!

Ian:

What city weighs a ton?

Barley:

That's easy!
New Mushroom<u>ton</u>!

What dangerous route is full of fruit?

The Path of Pear-il!

What swamps come in twos?
The Swamps of Des-*pair*!

What do you call a person with a sword who's upset about everything?
A mighty *worrier*!

Knock-knock!
Who's there?
Yore!
Yore who?
Yore going on
a quest!

Knock-knock!
Who's there?
I can Barley!
I can Barley who?
I can *Barley* keep
my eyes open, I'm
so tired!

Ian:

What do gnomes do after
they finish working?

Barley:

What else?
They go <u>gnome</u>!

Wacky Wizards

What's a wizard's favorite subject in school?

Spelling!

Ian:

Why did the wizard have so many people working for him?

Barley:

Because every wizard needs a staff!

What do wizards use to write?

Magic markers!

What do you call someone who does magic in the middle of winter?

A *blizzard*!

Ian:

How many wizards does it take to change a light bulb?

Barley:

Into what?

Ian:

Do wizards cast shadows?

Barley:

No, only spells!

Knock-knock!
Who's there?
Wiz!
Wiz who?
Wiz whom did you
wish to speak?

Why did Officer Bronco
arrest the wizard?

**Because she was on the
Most *Wanded* List!**

What did the
wizard feed
his cat?

**A *sorcerer*
of milk!**

What do you call a wizard
who asks a lot of questions?

A *quiz-ard* !

Manticore Mania

What did Corey call her
underground restaurant?

The Manticore's *Cavern*!

What do you call a manticore
who joins the police force?

A manti-*cop*!

What are manticores usually
in the middle of?

Manti-*apples*!

How do manticores prepare for quests?

They don't—they just wing it!

What do you call a manticore who's been flying for twenty-four hours?
Tired!

What's Corey's favorite vegetable?
Manti-*corn*!

What do you call a whole bunch of manticores?
Many-cores!

How do manticores like to eat their ice cream?
In manti-*cones*!

Why did the Manticore cross the road?
Because she Manti-*could*.

Dragon Distractions

What's hungrier than a dragon?
Two dragons!

Why do dragons like stories?
They appreciate a good *tail*!

What happens if you make Blazey wear heavy shoes?
She'll be *dragon* her feet around!

What's the difference between a red dragon and a green dragon?
The green one isn't ripe yet!

How did the dragon weigh itself?
By using its scales!

What does a fire-breathing dragon eat?
Anything it wants!

What's a dragon's favorite snack?
Firecrackers!

How do dragons breathe fire?
Through their mouths!

What happens when a dragon is excited?
It gets all fired up!

What do you call a dragon who eats a dozen trolls?
Full!

What's blue and has scales?
A frozen dragon!

Elf Escapades

What kind of cell phone pictures does Ian take?

Elfies!

What's the first thing Ian learned in kindergarten?

The *elf*-abet!

What do you call an elf who never shares?

Elfish!

What do you call elves who work for themselves?

Elf-employed!

What's Ian and Barley's favorite animal?

An *elf*-ant!

Ian:

What do you call a rich elf?

Barley:

Welfy!

How do you make an elf shake?

Add two scoops of ice cream and an elf!

What's an elf's favorite number?

Twelf!

Ian:

What do you call a sneaky elf?

Barley:

Stelfy!

Why did the elf run around the bed?

To try to catch some sleep!

Creature Features!

What does a one-eyed
creature use to tell time?

A cy-*clock*!

How does a troll get
from the top of a hill
to the bottom?

He *trolls* down!

Laurel:
I think Grecklin
was hungry.

Corey:
How could you tell?

Laurel:
She was goblin up
her dinner!

What do you call
a flying horse
with an upset
tummy?

Pega-sick!

Why doesn't Barley like to drive on the highway?

There are too many _troll_ booths!

What do you do if a troll falls asleep on her face?

You just _troll_ her over on her back!

What's a mermaid's favorite month?

Mer-May!

What's a satyr's favorite
day of the week?

Satyr-day!

What's the difference
between a turkey
and a goblin?

**One likes to gobble;
the other's
always *goblin*!**

Silly Sprites

Why couldn't the sprites find
their contact lenses?

Because they *Dew*-dropped
them on the floor!

What's Dewdrop's favorite
frozen treat?

A motor-*sicle*!

What do you call a baby sprite?

A sprout!

Why do sprites fly?

Because it beats walking!

Knock-knock!
Who's there?
A sprite says!
A sprite says who?
No, an owl says who!

Mustardseed: Why is your motorcycle laying on the ground?

Cobweb: Because it's two tired!

What do sprites turn on before they go to sleep?
A *sprite-light!*

(Even More) Elf Escapades

What do elves eat to stay in good shape?

Helf food!

What do you call an elf wearing earplugs?

Anything you want—he can't hear you!

Where do Ian and Barley
keep their books?
On she*lves*!

What type of seafood do
elves love to eat?
Sh-e*lf*-ish!

Ian:
Don't tell anyone
about Dad!

Barley:
I'll keep it
to mys<u>elf</u>!

Knock-knock!

Who's there?

Interrupting elf!

Interrupting elf wh—

Hi, I'm the interrupting elf!

Where does a
hundred-foot-tall
elf sit?

Outside!

What has four
hands, two faces,
and pointed ears?

**An elf holding
a clock!**

Knock-knock!

Who's there?

Elves!

Elves who?

Elves who like to knock on
doors for no good reason can
really get on your nerves!

Barley's Gut Busters

Ian:

How do you make a curse go away?

Barley:

Tell it you're not home!

Ian:

I think Officer Bronco has a sore throat.

Barley:

That's because he's a little <u>horse</u>!

What do you call a van that
isn't afraid of anything?
Guin-*no-fear*!

Why doesn't a spell book get cold?
Because it has a jacket!

Ian:

How come you never see any trolls
hiding in trees?

Barley:

Because they're really
good at it!

Why did the troll cross the
playground?
To get to the other *slide*!

Knock-knock!
Who's there?
Aloft!
Aloft who?
It's *"Aloft Elevar,"* not
"Aloft Who."

How do you
talk to a
giant ogre?
**Try using
big words!**

Ian:

Where would you find a Phoenix Gem?

Barley:

The same place you lost it!

Why do adventurers do so
well on tests?

**They're great at
answering questions!**

Ian:

Why are you taking a game to bed?

Barley:

I'm gonna play Quests
of <u>Snore</u>!

Path of Puns

Kagar:

Did your brother like the Path of Peril?

Ian:

Are you kidding? He won't stop <u>raven</u> about it!

What's worth more than a centaur?
A *dollar*-taur!

Ian:

What's the worst time of year
to visit the Bottomless Pit?

Barley:

Fall!

What does a wizard put on a
peanut butter sandwich?
Phoenix *jam*!

Ian:

Can we fit a karaoke machine in our house?

Barley:

There's not <u>mushroom</u> for one!

What kind of reptiles know how to cast spells?

Lizards!

What do you call
a hand towel
with one eye?
A *cy-cloth*!

Ian:

Did you hear about the satyr
who lost his left side?

Barley:

He's all
ri<u>ght</u> now!

Trash Unicorns

Why are unicorns such annoying drivers?

They use their horns too much!

How many unicorns does it take to change a light bulb?

One. Oh, I'm sorry, that's how many unicorns it takes to EAT a light bulb.

What should you do if a trash
unicorn eats your pencil?

Use a pen!

What do you call a trash unicorn
that turns red and bumpy?

A *rash* unicorn!

What kind of instrument does
a unicorn play?

A unique horn!

What do you call a small unicorn?

A *pony*-corn!

What kind of unicorns
love to swim?

Splash unicorns!

What's a trash unicorn's favorite
kind of muffin?

Uni-*corn* muffins!

What did the baby unicorn say
to the mom unicorn?

"Where's Pop corn?"

How do trash unicorns charge
their phones?

With a uni-*cord*!

Why are trash unicorn
jokes so goofy?
**Because they're
uni-*corny*.**

What does a
trash unicorn
wear to
school?
A uni-*form*.

Creature Features, Take Two

Knock-knock!

Who's there?

Goblin!

Goblin who?

Goblin *you*, if you don't give me something to eat!

Why aren't centaurs
good dancers?

**They have two
left feet!**

Why do trolls like to
play board games?

**They love to *troll*
the dice!**

Can mermaids bake cakes?

**Sure, they can *mer-make*
anything they want!**

What one-eyed creature always
takes deep breaths?

A *sigh*-clops!

What do you call a half man,
half horse who wants everyone
to pay attention to him?

The *centaur* of attention!

Why can't you
trust a griffin?

Because they're
mostly *lion*!

Why did the ogre eat
his homework?

**Because the
teacher said it was
a piece of cake!**

What do you call a giant flying
horse with wings?

Mega-sus!

Centaur Silliness

Where do centaurs go
when they get sick?

To the *horse*-pital!

When does a centaur eat dinner?

***Whinny* wants to!**

Ian:

What's as big as Officer Bronco
but weighs absolutely nothing?

Barley:

His shadow!

Ian:

What do you call a centaur on roller skates?

Barley:

Unstable!

What do you call a freezing police officer?

Colt Brrronco!

Ian:

How long does it take centaurs to brush their teeth?

Barley:

A hoof an hour!

Where do centaurs usually live?

On Mane Street!

Ian:

I smell something funny.

Barley:

It must be a <u>scent</u>-taur!

What has four legs and
likes to go camping?
A *tent-aur*!

Ian:

Why did Officer Bronco
wake up screaming?

Barley:

Because he had a nigh<u>tmare</u>!

What do you call a centaur who
lives across the street?
Your *neighhhbor*!